WALT DISNEY
Mickey's Christmas Carol

Based on the classic by Charles Dickens

Crown Publishers, Inc.,   New York

Library of Congress Cataloging in Publication Data Maniere, Michel 1948— Mickey's
Christmas Carol. Translation of: Le Noel de Mickey. At head of title: Walt Disney.
Summary: A retelling of the classic Christmas tale, with Walt Disney's cartoon characters
filling the lead roles. 1. Children's stories, French. [1. Christmas — Fiction. 2. Ghosts
— Fiction. 3. England — Fiction. 4. Animals — Fiction] I. Dickens, Charles, 1812-1870.
Christmas carol. II. Walt Disney Productions. III. Title. PZ7.M31268Mi 1984 □ (Fic)
84-9491 ISBN: 0-517-55525-5
10 9 8 7 6 5 4 3 2 1
First American Edition

In London it rains more often than it snows. But on the twenty-fourth day of December of one particular year, there was no fog or gloomy drizzle. Instead there were soft snowflakes that tickled your ears and a thick, white quilt on everything outside, not just on the rooftops but also on the edges of the windows and even on the smoking chimney tops. It was going to be a real Christmas.

Everyone was very happy. There was only one person not thinking of Christmas presents or turkey or pine trees, only one person who did not see the wreaths on the doors of the houses or the beautifully decorated windows. There was only one person in a grumpy mood: Ebenezer Scrooge.

4

Noel! Noel!
Blessed Day of Joy.
You are warm in your home.
Think of those who are cold.
Noel! Noel!
Blessed Day of Love.
Noel! Noel!
You have plenty to eat.
Think of those who are hungry.

"What is all that hullabaloo?" he muttered to himself.
"These singers will break my eardrums. All they do is ask me for money. If the poor are poor, so be it. If they want to be rich, let them do what I have done."

"Please, sir, have pity on the needy," pleaded a poor cripple.

"Help yourself and the Lord will help you," Scrooge answered. "At least if he feels like it," he added under his breath.

Because he was President of the bank Scrooge & Company, Scrooge was constantly followed by all the beggars in the village.

"Oh, why can't they leave me alone," grumbled Scrooge. "Being rich nowadays is no fun."

To save money Scrooge had only one employee, Bob Cratchit. He was the bookkeeper, but he also washed his employer's laundry. That's why Scrooge was carrying a big bag of dirty clothes on his way to the bank.

Previously, Scrooge had an associate, Jacob Marley. "A good sort," Scrooge said to himself each time he saw Marley's name on the sign at the bank. "Marley robbed widows, cheated orphans, and embezzled the rich — all that one must do to be a good banker." Alas, the poor man (in a manner of speaking) had passed away seven years before, on Christmas Day. There was not much money left for his funeral since he had insisted that most of his sizable fortune be buried with him. That's what his will said, and that's what was done. "May he rest in peace," muttered Scrooge.

Cratchit had been working since 5:00 in the morning, and he was freezing. Scrooge & Company did not heat its offices well. A Nice Muffler Is More Valuable Than a Piece of Coal was Scrooge's motto.

"It's true that a muffler can last a lifetime while a piece of coal burns itself up in minutes, but nothing is better than a little fire when your feet and ears feel like icicles," thought Cratchit.

Unable to stand the cold any longer, Cratchit finally decided to build a small fire. But he had hardly lifted the bucket of coal when he heard footsteps echoing through the corridor. It was Scrooge!

"Aha! I've caught you, you scoundrel! You are going to ruin me!" screamed the banker as he let his great bundle fall to the floor.

Luckily, Cratchit had managed to save the precious coal before it went into the fire.

"I wasn't building the fire for myself, sir; it was for my inkwell. The ink froze and I wasn't able to write," Cratchit explained.

The argument made sense, and once Scrooge had checked to see that Cratchit had indeed been telling the truth, he allowed him to burn a few pieces of coal.

"Now we were saying: 5 plus 5 plus 3,000 minus 34. I keep 15 and subtract 7," Scrooge muttered. The banker liked nothing better than to count his money. He touched it, weighed it, sniffed it, arranged it in piles, and polished it on the sleeve of his coat until it sparkled.

Cratchit went back to work, but his heart wasn't in it. He had something important he wanted to ask Scrooge, but he didn't dare.

The door suddenly opened with a crash.

"Good day, everyone — and Merry Christmas!" cried the newcomer.

"Hello, Mr. Fred, and Merry Christmas to you too!" exclaimed Cratchit, delighted to see him.

"Maybe Fred will help me," Cratchit thought.

And in fact . . . "Why, dear uncle, are you making poor Cratchit work on Christmas Eve?" asked Fred.

"And why not," responded Scrooge indignantly. "If we had to observe all the holidays, we would never have time for business."

"But tomorrow is Christmas," Fred persisted.

"And Christmas is a workday like all the others, you fool!" Scrooge answered.

Cratchit returned to his work, very discouraged.

"I came to invite you to our family dinner," said Fred.

"Family dinner! Family dinner! I'm eertainly old enough to feed myself!" roared his uncle. "Now, enough, you're wasting my time," Scrooge bellowed as he returned to his desk.

But his nephew held him back. "At least take this wreath; I made it myself. Please accept it with my love," Fred implored.

"Love! Love! You can wrap your love around your neck — and the wreath also," cried Scrooge.

With that, Scrooge grabbed the wreath and pushed it over Fred's head. Then he opened the door and shoved his nephew out of the office.

But Fred was stubborn. He hung the wreath on the doorknob and cried out one last time: "Merry Christmas, all the same!"

As soon as he was gone, two rather prosperous-looking gentlemen came into the bank. "Clients!" Scrooge gloated. "Let me take care of them, Cratchit!" he exclaimed as he rubbed his hands together, already picturing the piles of gold on his desk getting higher and higher. "Merry Christmas, sirs! What can I do for you?" he asked in his gentlest voice.

"Merry Christmas," responded the gentlemen in unison. "We are collecting alms for the poor. We just need a little money, and . . ,"

Scrooge jumped in anger, but quickly regained his
composure. "Gentlemen, if you give money to the poor,
no one will be poor anymore. And if no one is poor, there

won't be any more good deeds for you to perform. No, I really can't let that happen!" With that, he gave them the wreath.

"Hmm . . . " thought Cratchit, after the visitors had left, "this is not a good time to ask for a day off, though I did so much want to celebrate Christmas with my family!"

When the clock struck 7:00, Cratchit got up to leave.

"Not so quickly, you idler!" screamed Scrooge. "That clock is ten minutes fast; my watch says six fifty. But since you are almost ready to go, we'll let it pass just this once," Scrooge relented, adding, "and don't come in tomorrow. I'll have alms collectors coming here instead of clients, and I don't want to pay you for doing nothing."

Cratchit could hardly believe his ears, but he tried to act as if nothing unusual had happened. He simply picked up the laundry bag and closed the door.

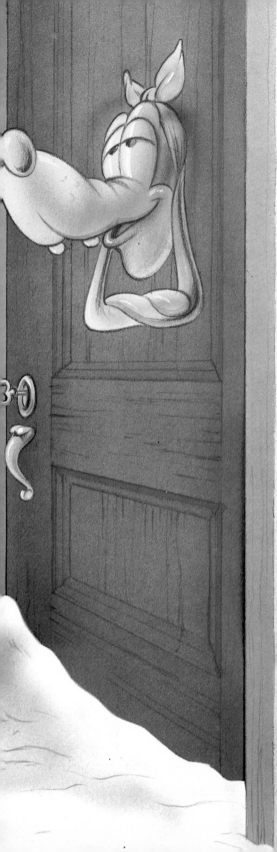

When Scrooge finally left his office to go home, it was very dark outside. The streets were deserted, and the snow was falling heavily. "Luckily I know the way home like the back of my hand," Scrooge said to himself. Even so, the familiar walk took him a long time, and when he reached his door Scrooge was tired and cold and not at all prepared for the awful shock he was about to receive.

Just as he was fitting his key into the lock, he saw something that made him jump back in horror. On the knocker, instead of the familiar face of an of an old lion, was the image of his former associate, Marley! Marley, who had been dead for seven long years. Scrooge was terrified.

Scrooge decided that he had two choices. He could either run away or he could compose himself long enough to get into his house and hide where no one would bother him. Without much hesitation, Scrooge entered the house.

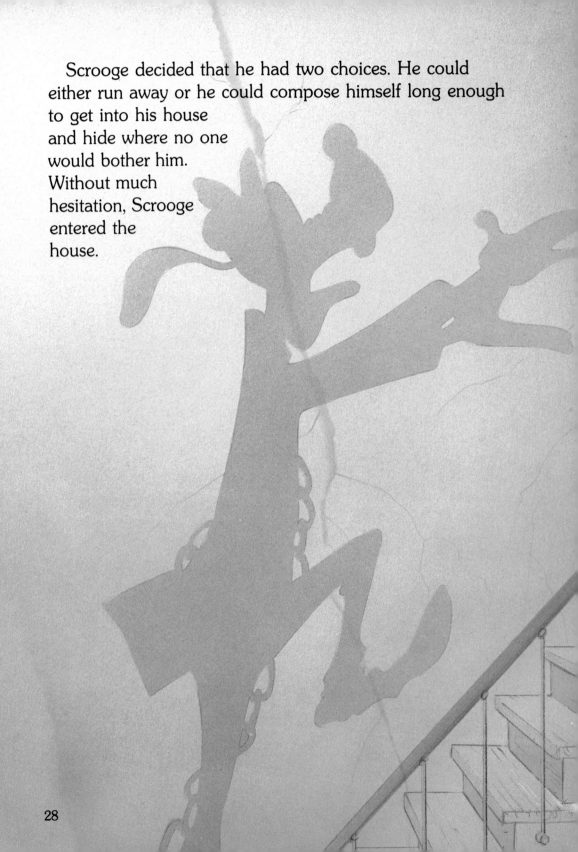

Once inside, Scrooge started up the stairs. Suddenly, he froze. He heard a terrible sound, like chains clanging. He turned around and, to his horror, saw the shadow of Marley on the wall. Scrooge screamed and ran as fast as his legs could carry him to the top of the stairs.

Scrooge dashed into his apartment and slammed the
door behind him. Though he was trembling from head to
toe, he somehow managed to bolt the three enormous
locks on his door. Feeling a little better, he gazed around
the room. The apartment was enormous, yet nearly empty.
The few pieces of furniture were covered by large, white
sheets and looked so much like ghosts that Scrooge began
to wish he had run away after all. To make matters worse,
he suddenly heard the chains clanging again, even more
loudly than before.

Scrooge's teeth began chattering. He knew that no door, no lock could ever keep a ghost away. "Tap, tap, tap," Scrooge heard.

Without waiting for an answer, the ghost entered the room. "Dear Scrooge!" it cried out. "You haven't forgotten your old friend Marley, have you? Yes, it's me, Marley, your old associate Marl . . . "

ZWACK! The ghost's entry was interrupted. By mistake he had put his foot on top of the cane Scrooge had left on the floor. The cane started rolling and Marley's foot began to slip ... ZI ... I ... I ... IP ...

Marley struggled to regain his balance ... WHAM! KAZAM! He began to fall.

He collapsed across Scrooge's sofa and practically squashed him. Marley's chains were attached to an enormous chest that luckily landed away from the couch — on the floor.

Scrooge and Marley got up. In all the excitement Scrooge had forgotten how frightened he was. "Marley, is it really you, you old devil? You certainly were less clumsy when I knew you. I don't believe death has improved you!" exclaimed Scrooge, smiling.

"Be quiet, Scrooge! You have nothing to laugh about! You don't understand. . . . Do you want me to tell you about this chest that almost fell on us?"

"But, it's the one we buried with you," Scrooge said, surprised.

"Exactly," responded Marley, ominously.

"And those are the keys," cried Scrooge, pointing. "What luck," he continued, rubbing his hands together, "we'll be rich!"

39

"Don't touch it, you fool," screamed Marley. "Do you know what's in that chest?"

"Your fortune, of course," answered Scrooge.

"How mistaken you are, my friend! All my past sins, all my wrongdoings, all my faults, and all my mistakes are in that chest! It's heavier to carry than all my gold, and I am doomed to carry it forever. I am doomed, my friend, doomed. And as for you, Scrooge, if you continue being such a scoundrel you will end up like me!" Marley warned.

Scrooge looked horrified; his eyes darkened as Marley lifted three terrible fingers in front of him.

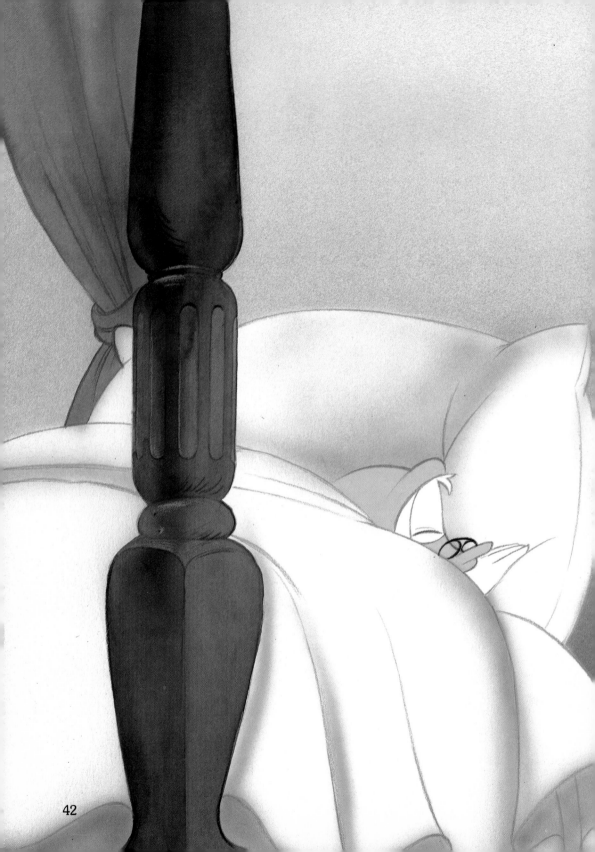

"Tonight, three ghosts will visit you," Marley told him. "Whatever you do, do not ignore them. This is your last chance, so listen carefully and do everything they say. Remember, it is your last chance!" Before Scrooge could reply, Marley had vanished.

"Oh, dear, what have I done?" Scrooge moaned. His teeth began chattering again. His hands and feet felt like icicles and his forehead began to throb. "I feel terrible," Scrooge groaned. And he quickly threw on his pajamas and buried himself under the covers.

He had not been asleep long when a shadow slowly began to glide across the bedroom wall. . . .

The shadow belonged to a tiny man wearing a funny blue hat and carrying an umbrella and gently knocked three times on Scrooge's alarm clock. Ding! Ding! Ding!

"Be brave, Scrooge, your hour has come," the shadow whispered.

Scrooge opened one eye.

"Come on, you must be more awake than that," said the little man.

"But who . . . who . . . who are you?" Scrooge asked, sleepily.

"I am the ghost of Christmas Past."

"But I would have thought . . . I would have thought . . . that you would be . . . that you would be bigger!" exclaimed Scrooge.

"Do not make fun of little men, Scrooge! Please remember, if we were to measure people by their kindness, you would be no larger than a grain of sand," answered the ghost.

Scrooge did not answer; he was too afraid. But he did wonder why the ghost mentioned kindness to him.

"After all, what does kindness have to do with anything," Scrooge wondered. He didn't have much time to think about it though, for his visitor suddenly seemed to be in a great hurry.

"Please hold onto me as best you can," the ghost advised. "We're going for a ride," he continued as he opened the window.

Scrooge clung to the little man's foot and felt himself being lifted up and carried away across the sky.

"Brr, it's cold," complained Scrooge.

"Why don't you enjoy the trip instead of moaning and trembling? It's not everyday that you can see the world from this high up," the ghost snapped.

"Why, that's Fizziwig's house!" exclaimed Scrooge once he had recovered from his rather rough fall into the snow.

"Yes . . ." agreed the ghost. (Thanks to his umbrella he was still in the air.)

"Do you remember?" the little man asked sadly.

"I do remember . . . it's true, Fizziwig was kind, as you say. It's all coming back to me now," murmured Scrooge.

"That's good, very good," said the ghost, a bit mysteriously. "Let's go closer to the house."

49

Scrooge pressed his nose against the windowpane. "But it's Isabelle; she looks so young, so pretty, so sweet, so . . . but . . . but the shy young man dancing with her under the mistletoe . . . that's me!" exclaimed Scrooge.

"You mean that *was* you!" said the ghost.

Scrooge looked distressed. "Have I changed that much?" he asked.

"Yes, you have indeed. You know, you were once kind and good, but that was long ago . . ."

"Before money corrupted you!" finished the ghost of the past.

"Look in the window now, and you'll see what I mean," the ghost ordered.

"But ... but that's my office ... and that's Isabelle. But why does she look so unhappy?" Scrooge asked.

"Why!" cried the ghost of the past. "Open your eyes and ears! You'll understand why!"

And little by little, Scrooge began to remember. It was as if he were there again.

"You promised to marry me," said Isabelle, "And that pretty house in the country that I had fixed up — it was for us both . . ."

"Yes, yes," muttered Scrooge, absentmindedly, as he counted his money. "Now let me see, you owe me twenty-three pounds, And as for the house, I've taken it; it's now mine to sell."

"I thought you loved me!" moaned Isabelle as she rushed away in tears.

"I certainly tricked her," Scrooge gloated.

But the Scrooge of today was not as pleased. "I should never have done that," he groaned.

"And yet you did," the ghost said sharply.

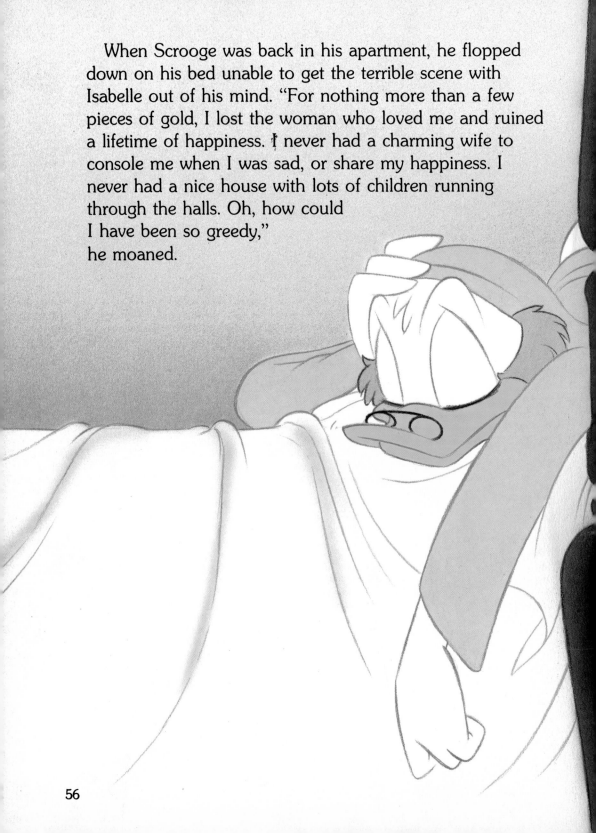

When Scrooge was back in his apartment, he flopped down on his bed unable to get the terrible scene with Isabelle out of his mind. "For nothing more than a few pieces of gold, I lost the woman who loved me and ruined a lifetime of happiness. I never had a charming wife to console me when I was sad, or share my happiness. I never had a nice house with lots of children running through the halls. Oh, how could I have been so greedy," he moaned.

"Oh, how I wish I could fall asleep! But I can't! Besides I probably shouldn't. Marley said two more ghosts would knock on my door."

"No, Scrooge, you have not become a dwarf! Besides, if we were to measure people by their sins, you would be larger than a mountain! But for now, I am the giant, the ghost of Christmas Present. Come here, so I can see you more clearly."

Scrooge was terrified as two enormous hands reached down to pick him up.

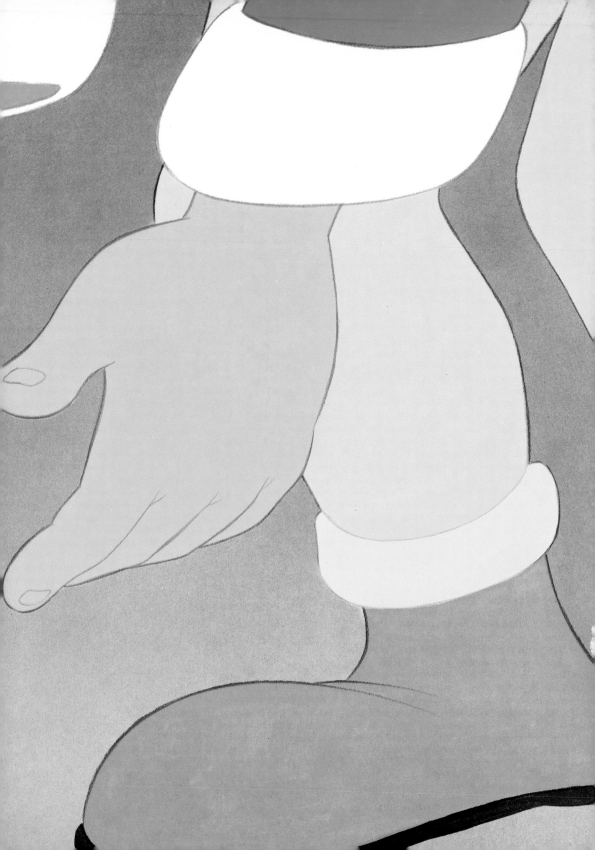

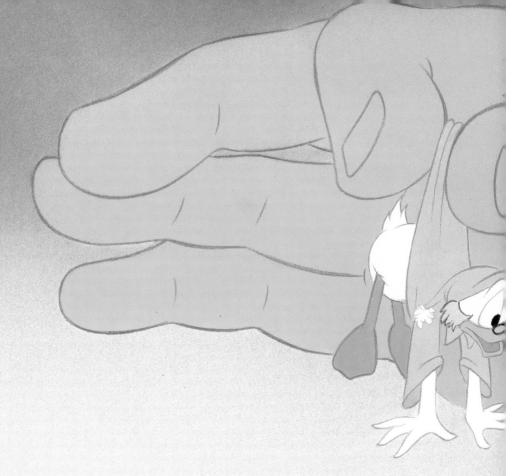

"What a little rat you are," muttered the giant
as he dangled Scrooge in front of his nose.

"Please, Mr. Giant, don't eat me!" Scrooge
pleaded.

"Now why would I want to eat you, you little crumb,
when there are so many delicious things I could have," the
giant replied. And with an amused expression he
proceeded to tell his terrified captive what he had eaten
for dinner the night before: a whole stuffed whale,
a herd of lamb on a single skewer, followed by
an avalanche of fresh fruit, and washed
down with enough chocolate milk to fill
the Atlantic Ocean.

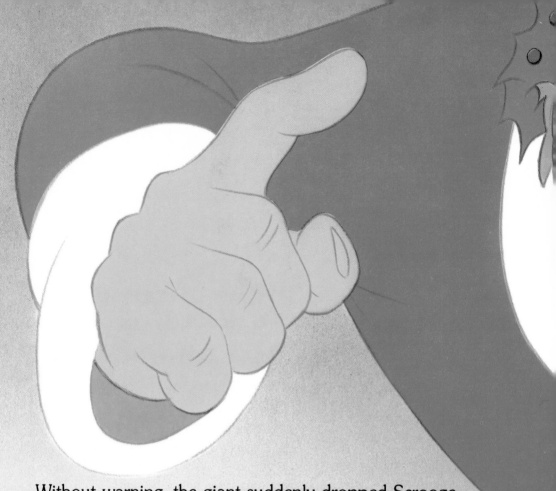

Without warning, the giant suddenly dropped Scrooge onto an enormous bowl of fresh fruit. He landed on a bunch of grapes and bounced from grape to grape as if they were giant balloons. Just as he appeared to have regained his balance, the giant picked up the grapes by the stem. Scrooge, bewildered, held on as best he could.

"Where does all this fruit come from, Mr. Giant?" asked Scrooge, clinging to a grape.

"From the heart, my friend, from goodwill and generosity — things you know nothing about, " the giant replied.

"Generosity?" repeated Scrooge, puzzled. "I've never heard anyone speak of it before."

Without answering, the giant suddenly picked Scrooge up and put him in his pocket. Then, since he was too big to go out by the front door, he lifted off the roof of the house and easily climbed over the wall. It was still very dark outside, so the giant snatched the first streetlamp he saw and carried it in one hand like a flashlight. And off they went.

Although Scrooge was nice and warm in the giant's pocket, he did not feel very safe.

"I wish I knew what was happening. We seem to be getting farther and farther away from the center of town. Where can we be going on a night like this?" Scrooge muttered to himself.

"We're here; you can come out now," the giant suddenly announced, interrupting Scrooge's thoughts.

Scrooge stepped out and found himself facing the smallest house he had ever seen. "Do shacks like this exist in London?" he exclaimed. "It looks like it could be the home of a tramp or one of those shabby beggars who are always asking me for money."

"Go closer," the giant ordered, pushing him toward the window with his finger.

"Why, it's Cratchit, my employee!" Scrooge was stunned.

"Yes, indeed, it's your employee," the ghost replied. "He can barely live on what you pay him, and in exchange he works more than fifteen hours a day helping you build your fortune. Is that what you call generosity?" The giant was furious.

"And look at what they are eating on Christmas Eve — a scrawny chicken!" exclaimed the giant.

"It isn't much," Scrooge admitted.

"But what is that over there, boiling in that enormous kettle?" Scrooge asked, pointing.

"Would you like to guess?" asked the ghost of Christmas present.

"I don't know . . . perhaps some pot roast, or stew or hmmm . . . soup?"

Each time the giant shook his head, no.

"YOUR LAUNDRY IS BOILING IN THAT ENORMOUS KETTLE," the giant finally screamed, totally exasperated. Scrooge hid his face, almost dying of shame.

When he looked up again, he saw a little boy approaching the table on crutches.

"Who is that?" Scrooge asked.

"Oh, that's Tiny Tim," growled the giant, "I'm afraid the poor child doesn't have long to live," he said sadly.

"What do you mean?" Scrooge asked, horrified.

"He's suffering from a serious disease; that's what I mean," the giant replied. "Maybe if he were under the care of a good doctor, he might get better. But, as you know, he is the son of poor parents who don't even have enough money to feed him properly. No, there's no hope. I'm sure he will die," the giant finished tearfully. A huge tear fell on Scrooge who dried himself off as best he could and continued to look through the window.

"What's happening?"
Scrooge suddenly exclaimed.
"Why are they all so
unhappy?"

But the ghost did not
answer. He remained
speechless, his mouth open,
starring through the window,
even more dumbfounded than
Scrooge.

"Tiny! ... Tiny! ... Tiny
Tim! ... " repeated Scrooge,
shouting like a madman. Soon
Scrooge could not even hear
his own voice as a terrifyingly
loud din of funeral bells rang
through the night. They were
so loud, Scrooge was sure they
could be heard around the
world.

Then, smoky clouds began to form near the ground. The giant disappeared, and Scrooge felt himself being lifted into the air. Suddenly the tolling bells became even louder.

"Help! Help me!" Scrooge screamed. "Mr. Giant, where are you? Where are you? I need help! Please, he . . . l . . . p. . . ."

Scrooge was barely able to finish his sentence when the smoke got into his mouth and throat. He knew he was about to sneeze.

The silence that followed was so deep, so strange, and so stirring that Scrooge almost believed it was his sneeze that had stopped the tolling bells. As he looked around him, he saw gravestones, tombs and a small chapel all covered with snow. He was in a cemetery in the dead of night.

"And over there . . . what is that?" Scrooge asked. "It's moving; it's ENORMOUS!!!"

The monster was indeed enormous. He lit a cigar and said, "Are you looking for someone, Sir? Can I help you?"
Though the monster sounded kind, Scrooge did not feel too confident. With his slanted eyes, crooked smile, and huge frame, the monster was hardly a reassuring sight. And yet, what if he were . . .

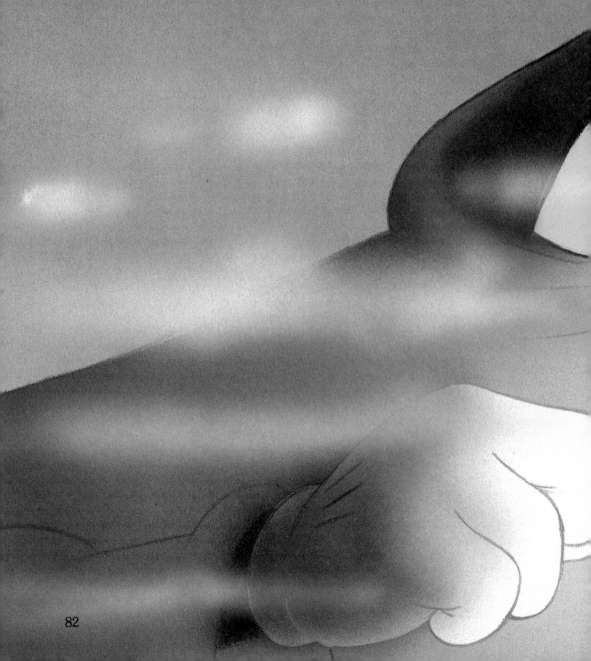

"You must be the ghost of Christmas yet to come,
the ghost of the future," Scrooge said.

When the monster did not answer, Scrooge thought
he had insulted him. He was about to excuse himself
when suddenly he changed his mind. "Yes, I am
looking for someone," Scrooge found himself saying. . . .
"A little boy . . . Tiny Tim."

Without uttering a word, the monster lifted an
enormous arm and pointed to a grave in the distance.

Scrooge started to walk in the direction the monster had indicated, but suddenly stopped, stunned. The grave in question was newer than the others. Cratchit was standing over it holding Tiny Tim's crutch in one hand and looking sadder than Scrooge had ever seen him. His grieving wife and children were behind him. Scrooge tried to say something to comfort them but was interrupted by loud tolling bells ringing to announce a funeral. The earth trembled under him. He put his hands over his ears and closed his eyes.

When he finally reopened his eyes, it was very quiet. The
monster was still there, calmly smoking his cigar. To his
horror, Scrooge noticed the open grave at his feet.

"Mr. Monster," Scrooge implored, "tell me that this isn't
true. Tiny Tim can't be dead, not yet, that this grave . . ."

"This grave!" a voice sniggered behind him.
Scrooge turned around, but saw no one.

"This grave!" repeated a voice on his right.
Again there was no one there.

Then on his left—"This grave!"

"This grave!" he heard. He turned,
this time not surprised to find no one.

Scrooge bent over the grave thinking that perhaps the terrible voice was coming from underneath the ground. "Is anyone down there?" he asked timidly.

"Not yet, not yet, but it won't be long before someone will be," said a mysterious voice.

This time Scrooge was sure it was the monster who had answered him. He was about to turn around when he felt a huge hand on his neck.

"I believe that this grave is meant for you, Scrooge!" he heard the voice say. And before he could think of what to do, he felt himself being pushed into the grave.

"Help me, please! Someone, help me!" Scrooge screamed.

The grave seemed like a bottomless pit. While he was falling he saw all the people he had ever known passing in front of him: the beggars he took such pride in snubbing, the alms collectors he threw out of his office, his betrayed fiancee and, last of all, poor Cratchit and his family. They were all looking at him reproachfully.

"Oh, help me! Please, someone have pity on me! I'll be better, I promise! I'll never rob or cheat any of you again! Never! Never!"

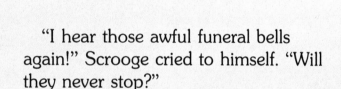

"I hear those awful funeral bells again!" Scrooge cried to himself. "Will they never stop?"

Then suddenly, everything changed. The bells became softer and more pleasant. Scrooge half-opened his eyes.
"Why it's a miracle! I'm in my room! I'm at the foot of my bed!" he exclaimed. "And the bells . . ."
He got up and ran to the window. "The bells aren't announcing a funeral; they're ringing for Christmas. It's Christmas morning!" Scrooge was overjoyed. "My third visitor must have been the ghost of the future. If I'm right, that means Tiny Tim is still alive. Hurray!"

Scrooge grabbed his hat and coat and rushed out of the house. "There's not a minute to lose," he cried. "I must get to the Cratchits'!"

He had not gone very far when he saw the two gentlemen who had walked into his bank the day before.

"Merry Christmas, my dear sirs," Scrooge said warmly. "I hope your business is going well," he added.

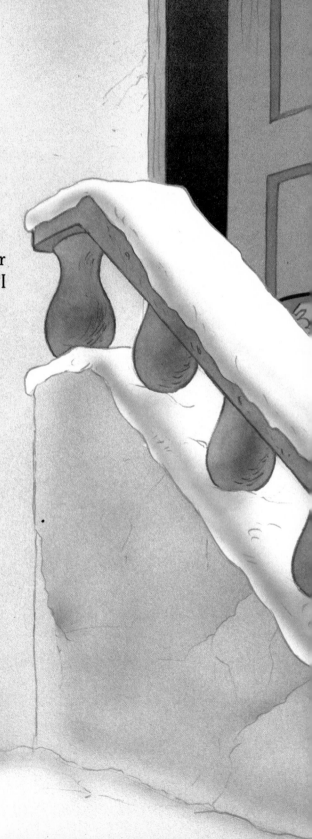

"Please allow me to give you something too — here."
And before the bewildered gentlemen could recover,
Scrooge began tossing gold coins into their tin cup. "For
the orphans and the invalids," he said as he handed them
two more bags of gold.

"But this is too much, Mr. Scrooge," said the gentlemen
in unison.

"Oh, it's Christmas! Please just accept these gifts with
my blessing," Scrooge said as he ran off.

A few feet down the road, Scrooge saw the carolers he had heard that morning. He rushed over to wish them all a Merry Christmas and quickly departed, singing at the top of his lungs. Just as he was finishing the carol, he spied his nephew, Fred, driving his carriage down the road.

"Why, hello, Fred — Merry Christmas!" Scrooge called out as he hurried over to the carriage.

"I hope the turkey is well cooked, Fred. I just have one small matter to take care of first, but afterward, I plan to be over for that Christmas dinner you promised me. I'm looking forward to it; it was very kind of you to invite me."

Fred and the horse stared at Scrooge, flabbergasted.

Carrying an enormous bundle over his shoulder,
Scrooge finally knocked on Cratchit's door. Cratchit came
to the door, followed by Tiny Tim.

"Why, Mr. Scrooge, please come in," exclaimed Cratchit.

"Would . . . would you please stay for supper?" Cratchit
asked not knowing what else to say.

"I don't have time, my friend," Scrooge answered,
brandishing his cane. "I've brought you more dirty laundry,
and I want it washed right away!"

"But it's Christmas, Mr. Scrooge!" protested Mrs. Cratchit, coming into the room.

Scrooge turned to face her. At the same time, a little teddy bear accidentally slipped out of his pocket.

"Oh, look at that," cried Tiny Tim, pointing the bear out to his little sister. The little girl was delighted. She had only seen stuffed animals behind store windows. If only she could take this one, and touch it — just once!

She was about to reach for the bear when suddenly
Scrooge turned around, looking furious. But instead of
screaming at her, as she had thought he would, Scrooge
placed his huge bundle in front of her and ordered all the
children to open it.

The children had never seen so many presents. Giggling and laughing they carried the parcels over to the Christmas tree and began to open them.

"A doll! Oh, thank you, Mr. Scrooge!"

"A tambourine! Oh, thank you, sir!"

"A rocking horse! I have always wanted one."

The children ran over and gave Scrooge a big hug.

"Come to dinner, everyone!" Mrs. Cratchit called out.

"Mr. Scrooge has also brought us a beautiful turkey and some plum pudding! Come to dinner while it's still hot!"

Please stay and have supper with us, Mr. Scrooge," said Cratchit, this time meaning every word.

"I would, it's just that Fred, my nephew . . . hmm." But Scrooge didn't hesitate for long. "Oh, after all, they'll wait for me. I'd love to stay and have supper with you," he decided.

"Two good meals in one evening isn't too much when it's Christmas," Scrooge added. The Cratchits agreed.

"Long live Mr. Scrooge," they all cried.

"And long live my teddy bear," added the little girl.

After dinner, while he was resting in the rocking chair surrounded by the grateful family, Scrooge announced that he would triple Cratchit's salary and the next month would make him his partner.

"Now you will have money for doctors," Scrooge said. "And I promise you that by next Christmas, Tiny Tim will be cured," he assured them.

Upon hearing this, Cratchit and his wife wept for joy, and Scrooge soon had tears in his eyes as well.

"Oh, it's so good to be kind and generous," Scrooge cried. "A MERRY CHRISTMAS TO ALL!"